E   Morrison, Bill
MOR
     Louis James hates
     school

DATE DUE

Morrison, Bill		E MOR
AUTHOR		
Louis James hates school		
TITLE		

DATE LOANED	BORROWER'S NAME	DATE RETURNED
10-31	Lia Kueck	C
11-8	caine	C
1/9	paul	B

THE BAKER & TAYLOR CO.

Louis James Hates School

Written and Illustrated by
BILL MORRISON

Houghton Mifflin Company Boston 1978

Library of Congress Cataloging in Publication Data

Morrison, Bill, 1935-
  Louis James hates school.

  SUMMARY: A young boy learns the value of formal
education when he quits school to find a job.
  [1. Dropouts—Fiction] I. Title.
PZ7.M82925Lo   [E]   78-60496
ISBN 0-395-27156-8

Louis James Hates School

Louis James skipped school again.
He hid behind the old elm tree until
everyone went inside. He hated school.
He hated everything about school
except gym and recess. And because
he was out so much, he never learned
to read or spell like his friends.

Put
Trash
Here

"Who needs to learn
those dumb things," said
Louis James. "I'm going to get
a job today and make a lot of money. I'll buy a
mini-bike and a racing car, and I'll be so busy
I won't have time to read books and spell stuff."
Into the trash went his books, and Louis James
headed for town to find a job.

He went to see the man who gave out jobs.

Louis James waited patiently while Mr. Klinker, the
head job-person, shuffled through a pile of papers.
"Can you read and spell, young man?"
"Of course," lied Louis James.
"Here's a good one," Mr. Klinker said, pulling a paper from
the file drawer.

"The ABC Skywriting Company needs a pilot to fly their plane and write smoke messages in the air. Can you handle that?"
"It's a snap," said Louis James.

Soon he was flying high over the town. His boss, who was sitting behind him, shouted, "Your job is to write EAT CRISPY COOKIES. Press the smoke button and make nice big letters so that everyone on the ground can read them."
Louis James tried his best, which was not very good.
"You are fired!" his boss shouted. "Who ever heard of a skywriter who can't spell?"
Louis James landed the plane and walked back to town.
He hurried to the Job Place.

"Flying doesn't seem to agree with me, is there something else I can do? Something without spelling. It's such a bore." Mr. Klinker shuffled through more papers.

"Here's one, someone to drive an ambulance."

"An ambulance driver!" shouted Louis James.

"That's great. Lights flashing, siren on, beep-boop, beep-boop, beep-boop,

R-R-R-R-R-R-R . . . . . . now that's for me!"

16

Soon he was driving down Main Street, with a lady in
back bandaged from head to toe.
"Get me to the hospital as quickly as you can, young man.
I hurt all over," she said.
"I don't know the way," said Louis James.
"Well, just follow the signs," said the lady
impatiently. "You can read, can't you?"

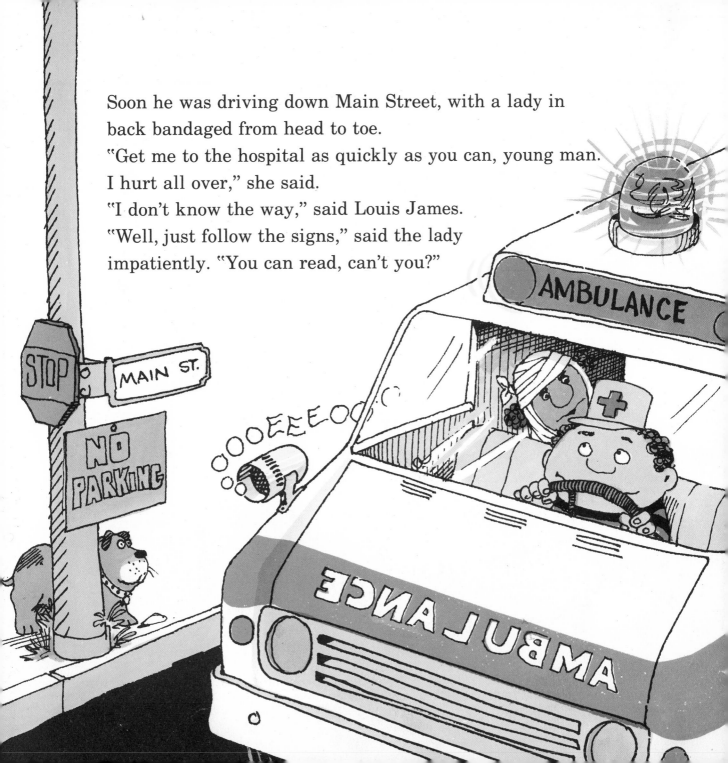

Louis James didn't answer.
He sped down the street, siren on
full blast. There were signs at every
corner and signs along the road, but
he could not tell what they said.
He came to a crossroad. The signs
pointed left and right.
He turned right.

BRUCE
MAIN ST.
MAIN ST.
BRUCE RD.
TO THE BEACH
TO THE
HOSPITAL
SLOW

"Where are you going?" shouted the woman in the back.
"That sign said to turn left for the hospital."
"I'm sorry, but I can't read," said Louis James very softly.
"Get out!" she screamed. "I'll drive myself."

And she did.

He went to see the head job-person once again.
"So you can't read or spell," said Mr. Klinker.
"I suggest you go back to school and forget
about a job for now."
"No!" shouted Louis James. "I hate
school. I'll never go back. Just
get me a job with no reading
or spelling. There must
be something I can do."
So Louis James
tried many
jobs.

DON'T
ASK

21

Night Watchman in a haunted house.

Spinach Taster in the Popeye Spinach Factory.

Snake Snuggler in a Side Show.

Tooth and Fang Brusher at the Zoo.

Pea Picker.

Pickle Packer.

Prune Peeler.

Louis James ran all the way back through town. He ran past
the Job Place where Mr. Klinker watched from the window.

"I'll be back for one of those good jobs," shouted Louis James.
He didn't stop until he reached the trash barrel in front of
the school.

Louis James pulled out his books,
brushed them off,
took the top book and
turned to page one.